I SEE YOU!

A Poetic Experience

Isaac Brown Jr

Published in New Castle, Delaware by 4Streams Series, LLC

LCCN: 2021900524
ISBN: 978-1-7363362-0-5

Individuals described in the poetry are composites drawn from multiple individuals and situations. Any resemblance to actual persons alive or dead is a coincidence.

Ordering Information
Books may be purchased in large quantities at a discount for educational, business, or sales promotional use. For information, email ikeseesyou@ gmail.com.

Project Management: Spoonfed Motivation Publications
Author Image and "I See Your Denial" Image Photographer: Ikeya S. Brown
All other images taken by the author, Isaac Brown Jr.

I SEE YOU!

A Poetic Experience

Isaac Brown Jr

4Streams Series, LLC

Dedication, Acknowledgments, & Inspirations

This book is dedicated to my beautiful and brilliant wife, Cynthia Lynn Brown, whose encouragement and faith in me provided the fuel that charged my creative energy!

Special thanks to my beautiful and brilliant daughter, Ikeya Simone Brown, who along with Cynthia, provided encouragement and constructive critiques generated by several reviews of this book. Thank you, most of all, to my Lord and Savior Jesus Christ whose grace and mercy have kept, guided, and blessed me throughout my life!

The poems in this book were inspired by conversations, observations, and personal experience with friends and strangers. Though individuals may have inspired the poetic concepts, some, if not most, are a synthesis of several people and situations.

I encourage you to not only read them for yourself but read them aloud in front of your friends and associates.

Table of Contents

A LOOK
INTO THE PAST

I Remember

I remember a time when people
Cared so much more about each other
Neighbors treated neighbors
Like their best flavor of ice cream
Chocolate, Vanilla, or Swirl
It used to be such a different world

But now folks hide behind solid-walled fences
Made for privacy
As I wonder
How will I know the neighbors
That I cannot see

So now we barely speak
When we walk out the door
And if someone bothers to say hello
We wonder if that stranger
Wants something more

You see our parents used to borrow
 Sugar and flower from one another
And made cookies and cake from scratch
And shared it with each other

They never had to ask twice
Or even say please
They looked out for each other
Even sharing powdered milk
And government cheese

But now some people don't want to share
A penny on a dollar
They are so afraid someone
Will have more than them
That they sweat until
They have ring-around-the-collar

I remember the block parties
When we used to lock down the whole street
And the air was filled with love, music,
Fried chicken and other delicious treats

As kids we stayed outside
All day long
Playing jump rope, 1-2-3 red light
Or hide and go seek
Unlike today's world
Where families cocoon themselves
With cell phones and computers
And make no time to speak

I remember a time
When I was a kid

And when I messed up
There was no place
I could have hidden
Because my neighbors
Made me confess up
When I did things
That were forbidden
But now, if you try to correct another's child
They are liable to cuss you out
As their parents tell you to
Mind your own business
And get the you know what out

In my time
Respect was given to anyone
Older than my age
And I would not even think about
The things some of today's kids say in their rage
My parents did not spare the rod
If I got out of place
A branch from a nearby tree
Often stated their case

Though when I got a beating
It really wasn't that hard
Even if it was an electrical cord
So I would fake a cry
And think, thank you Lord

And unlike today
Where some parents
Say to their kids
I'm going to church
Do you want to go

Our parents said
Put on your Sunday's best
You're going to church
And you better not be slow

But I developed discipline and
Respect for others that I never lost
And even in my wildest days
The seeds that were planted
Created lines that I never crossed

I know that the past is the past
There is no need to fuss
But I like to remember
That the foundation has been laid
To make things better for all of us

She Used to Be My Lady

When I looked into her eyes
I saw the sleepiness
Of a life gone wrong
Even so time could not erase
The strong woman she once was

There was still a trace of beauty
In eyes surrounded by wrinkles
Though her smile still sprinkled
With sadness

She was ashamed but glad to see me
Though I had forgotten her name
She remembered mine

But all I could remember
Was how fine she used to be
You see
She used to be my lady

But now her breath smelled like
Bitter beer mixed with the vomit of yesterday's meal
Still she smiled freely
Because she was glad to see me

Though I could not help but to notice
Huge spaces in a once sultry mouth
Now surrounded by hash brown-colored teeth

But as I walked past her
She moved her hips with just enough flair
To cause me to stare and remember
She used to be my lady

I wonder what happened to her
What lies within the book of her life
What lies does she now run from
The chapters written
But not known to me
Her hidden pages
Awaken my curiosity
Did she suffer from abuse
Was it sickness
Love lost but never found
Was there a baby never born for her touch

She used to be on solid ground
She used to be loved so much
You see she used to be my lady

We used to go to upscale places
Everywhere with her was my fairytale oasis
She's the one who taught me manners and etiquette
Helped me to remember the things I used to forget

But now she doesn't remember enough of
How she used to be
To even be ashamed of how she is
But I remember and she remembers me
Because she used to be my lady

Love Don't Hurt
and Hurt Don't Love!

I knew her brothers
And her brothers knew me
She was the only girl in a dysfunctional family
I'll call her Betty
To protect her anonymity

Her father beat her mother
Even cut her mother in the face
But her mom thought leaving him
Would be a much bigger disgrace

So Betty and her brothers
Had to witness that horrible sin
Papa beating momma
Over and over and over again
And each time her daddy hit her mother
He'd say he was sorry
But Betty and her brothers knew he was sorry
He was a sorry mother fa–courageous
In beating the defenseless

So now her brothers drink
And some have done time
And Betty thinks that love
Is just a nursery rhyme
Unkind and of not much worth
Cause she don't know
Love don't hurt
And hurt don't love

I ran into Betty one day in town
Betty is a grown-up woman now
She had a made-up face to hide a black eye
And a made-up story
To hide the reasons why

She said
At least when her boyfriend hits her
It shows he cares
But in the midst of our conversation
Both of us were hiding tears

My mind flashed back to an earlier time
When Betty saw her mother
Broken with hopeless hope
And paralyzed with fear

And I feel so sad that
Betty doesn't know her own worth

And just like mom and dad
She repeats the curse

Because She don't know
Hurt don't love
And
Love don't hurt

That's My Girlfriend

I was walking down the street
With I guy I hardly knew
He looked extremely irritated
So with a slight cough
I looked him in the eye and said
What did I do

Apologetically he said
It's not you my brother
It's my girlfriend

She's been messing around
Got her clothes laid all over town
She's been here and been there
There has been many a place
She has left her underwear

She's got people paying for her rent
And paying for her home
And when the money is all spent
She's ready to roam

Then I said hey brother
She can't be that bad
Maybe it just seems that way right now
Because you are so mad

Ignoring me he angrily said
I'm tired of this shit
I can't make pretend
It is time for me to git
And find another girlfriend

So I said brother
I am all ears
If you want to talk some more
We ain't doing anything but
Walking to the store

But he looked at me
And continued to call her a whore
But when he described her physical traits
I said hold up partner
Seems like you are describing
The same woman that I date

He did not even try to object
He just stuttered
And tried to cha-cha-change the subject

But I was fuming inside
And as my heart began to melt
I tried to hide all the awful things
I thought and I felt

Still I looked him dead in the eye
And said
Look bro I can't make pretend
You need to shut the hell up
Because the woman you previously described
Well
That's my girlfriend
Then I just walked the other way
Thinking that if I ever seen her again
I would never say to her or anyone else
That's my girlfriend

Years later
She got married and true to form
She ran on her husband
Until his heart was torn
Then he shot her lover
And brought his life to an abrupt end

Now he is in jail
And somebody else is telling his wife
That's my girlfriend

The Highway

As I rode down the highway
I looked at a poorly shaven man
Gently holding a sign
That read "Will work for food"

Many cars flew past
Going ever so fast
So they would not have to see
The lost expression on his face
And the grace they could give
To help him to live
Just a little bit better

Perhaps it was guilt
Or curiosity
But on this cold and bitter day
I assumed that the person
Who was supposed to stop
Was me

He held out a wrinkled hand
That seemed empty with hope
And needing some soap

To wash off the dirt
Of a lifetime trying to cope
In all the wrong ways

Though I did not really know
How his story went
My privileged self
Had the gumption to
Make the assumption
That he was derelict
In losing his way

And as I watched him flash his sign
I wondered if I had misjudged him
Just to ease my mind

I looked through my
Thick wallet
And wrestled with not knowing
That if I gave him money of any kind
Would it be used to fill yesterday's hunger
Or buy today's favorite cheap wine

As these thoughts danced in my mind
I kept my wallet in my pants
And pulled in secret

As I grasped a five-dollar bill
I hoped that I would not regret

That I would be
An enabler of habits that would kill

As I greeted him
I could not avoid staring at his afflictions
But I was convicted by the tormenting thought
Did I really care about his condition

Was this an act of false love
One that honors attachments to things
That belong to me
But denies the joy that true love brings
When you really connect with humanity

Not wanting to explore the answer
Or the price of my own remorse
I handed him a few more dollars
Which caused me to feel like
 I was paying for a bad divorce

Making no time for conversation
I drove off in my shiny car
Turned on my favorite song on my CD
Then hollered loud and clear
God bless you brother
And take it easy

But as he disappeared
In my rear-view mirror

My guilt deepened in a profound way
And I asked myself
Could I have helped him for a lifetime
Not just a day

I pulled off in such a hurry
That I rode past two other people
On the side of the highway
Though I was able to convince myself
That they were going to be okay

But God was not about
To set my guilt free
He said
If it was not for His grace and mercy
Those poor souls I rode pass
Could have been me

But still I kept riding
Praying for the courage to stop
And the wisdom to appreciate
Everything that I got

Plus the discipline not to
Judge others in any way
No matter where they are
Along life's highway

The Du-rag Man

It was several years ago
But I remember seeing him walk the streets
Lost in thoughtless thoughts that played through his head
Over and over again like a scratched twice CD

A stained rag tied tightly on a hairless head
Towered over a gaunt face
He looked like the walking damned
His was my old friend
The du-rag man

He walked and talked like a man with no mission
But in his heart he was
Always wishing
Wishing for a break wishing for a dime
Wishing he did not quit school
Wishing things would be different in time

He wished that he did not hurt
The ones who loved him so dearly
He wished he had the time
To slow down and really hear me

He was a fast talker
Though slow to speak
And each time we would meet
It was always the same phrase
What you got for the head
So one day I startled him and said
Knowledge my friend knowledge

But his mind was always moving too fast to hear
For he was always processing what
He
Wanted to say
So he repeated with a loud shout
What you got for the head
You know
What I'm talking about

Always stuck in time
Remembering how things used to be
He never took the time
To know how things should be

Unfortunately
He didn't even know his own self
He walked in pain but cried a silent cry
So his cries for help
Were never heard

Thus they became tormenting thoughts
Trapped in the subliminal world
Of no tomorrows
Where only his inner spirit knew
The depth of his sorrows

His smiles were an oxymoron of
Happy pain
For you see he believed
That he deserved to be in pain
Pain brought him in touch
With his own demons
And a chance to exorcise the past mistakes
That he had internalized all his life

And in his dysfunction
That
Made him feel good

Even so
He lived in a world where true peace
Was always in remission
Predicated on the condition
That he felt he never deserved to be at peace

He tried to counter
The unhappiness of his spirit
By indulging in spirits

But he was a drunken fool
Who fooled only himself

He bore the smile of a child
A smile that surely he would not have
If he knew how others really saw him
For their laughter was not filled with love

It was an acidic laughter
Filled with meanness
Meant to vaporize the lives
Of those who did not fit the click
Wicked laughter meant to destroy
And never to be enjoyed

So was the plight of the du-rag man

He was yesterday's cool
Never been schooled in
What's happening now
He prowled around town
Looking dated as a used dollar bill

He had the smell of unwashed clothes
Brought from Goodwill Industries
Or perhaps the Salvation Army

Either way
He looked like what used to be
What was
And what ain't any more

But he didn't know
Didn't even understand
And when I asked him to at least
Remove the rag off his head
He proudly said
Hell no
I am the Du-rag Man

I SEE YOUR
DENIAL

A Small-Town Story

It was a day not recorded
But remembered by some
The damned were raised upon
The land of the poor
Unleashing a flood of drugs
That turned neighborhoods
Into streets that resembled slums

At first it was about the money
Then about the power
In between
The people got devoured
And respect of the people
Got appropriated
By those who did not appreciate it

To my recollection
It started when the jobs went away
Factories that provided economic protection
Left the small town for states
That provided better tax breaks

Financial risks were too high
And profits were too low
The townsfolk were laid off so fast
It created a brand new status quo

The resources dissipated
And a socioeconomic storm
Formed a new norm for some
Take before you get taken or
Run before you get run over
Anything to survive
Do anything just to stay alive

Slumlords took advantage
Of those who could not afford
To live in a better place
Which made roach-infested
Low standard housing commonplace
Roofs leaked with rains
That were meant for vegetation
As the bum lords turned their backs
On the people's trepidation

Many slum lords were from
Distant and foreign lands
Who before they came to America
Were at the lower tier of a caste system
That treated them like
They were less than a man

Some begged on dirt road streets
For the bare essentials
But in this small town
They became proud owners
Of substandard rentals

They took advantage of the poor
And chose riches over right
As they rented houses
That they themselves did not like

The city refused to give many honest investors
A reasonable price to buy houses
That could be made nice enough to live in
They would rather see homes collapse
Before they would give in

The struggling town got worse
As the years moved on
Wind-blown trash replaced manicured lawns
Many people moved out of the small town
And as the population decreased
So did the opportunities

A whole host of issues
Flooded the area
Many became complacent
Which hid the mass hysteria
And even wisdom from the town elders

Could not erase it
Young pregnancies were not rare
And many children were raised
By young mothers
Who were still under
Their mothers' care
Grown up boy fathers
Took very little responsibility
Some did not bother to visit their kids
Others treated them like refugees

Some dropped out of school
Before they completed their education
Some left town for better accommodations
For those who stayed
Things got worse
It was as if the whole town
Was under an awful curse

Even today if you looked deep
Into the eyes of those walking the streets
You will see something missing
Like the walking damned on cable TV

Politicians made promises unfulfilled
Then the predators swooped in
To sell their drugs and pills

Crime increased and got so bad
That some of the police
Turned in their badge
Others were so afraid
That they refused to patrol
Many of the streets
It was rumored that local gangs
Took over their beat

Dilapidated projects were replaced
With encampments called section eight
Where citizens were given food stamps
To control what they ate
While rent was so low
It made the homes they lived in
Very hard to appreciate

There were no more grocery stores
Only dollar stores that provided
Inferior nutrition
Many turned to alcohol and drugs
To medicate their condition

The drugs came in such a huge tide
That the good people of the town
Were afraid to go outside

Then opportunist made a bad situation
Much worse

They used survival of the strongest
To justify the hurt
People used to fight with their fist
And then be friends the very next day
Now they primarily use guns
To blow their homies away

They have forgotten everyone
Is a homie in a small town
But sons and daughters of friends
Shoot each other now

They fight for territory
They do not own
And spend their drug money
On rent rather than buying a home

With all the crime in the streets
Homicides have increased
And these untimely deaths
Cannot be blamed on just the police
Because they are shooting each other
At a rate beyond belief

It is not race or ethnicity
That is to blame
Others living in such poverty
Have done the same

It's just that the news uses
Distortion reporting
To help win the ratings game

Those looking in from the outside
Have become unsympathetic
Attributing actions of the people
To unscientific genetics
But it's just an excuse not to help
Those less fortunate than themselves

Still there is a nucleus of believers
That have mustered enough faith
To believe the small town will rebound
At least that's what they say
To convince themselves to keep sticking around

Flashback

My friend and I had just left my cousin's place
He had smoked some dope
And I had sipped a little wine
I told him I could drive
But he said he was fine

So I slipped in a tape
Because I knew
It was going to be a long drive
But he ejected it
Then he punched me
On the blind side

It happened so fast
I thought it was an accident
But there I was
Punched in the eye
By one of my best friends
And it didn't make sense
At first
I did not know it was he that hit me
Until he cried like a baby and said

I'm sorry, I'm sorry
Please forgive me

Instinctively
My first urge was to punch him
In his eye
But then I thought
If I hit him
Who is going to drive

So there I was
Stuck on a major highway
And under a major attack
Cause my friend had a flashback
And brought his anger my way

When we got back home
He shared his life story
Then he began to cry
and once again
He apologized

It was then
That I looked my friend
Straight in the face and said

I am glad you apologized
But let us make a pact
And don't question me why

The next time you have a flashback
Don't be flashbacking
In my motherfuck'n eye

A Drug Story, Part I

I used to think the neighborhoods
That looked like shanty towns
Were the only places where drugs were found

That was until I witnessed
A young friend of mine go astray
It was many years ago
But I remember him
As clear as if it were today

He was upper-middle class
And came from a good family
Even went to college and got A's and B's

He could have been a great leader
And reached for the sky
But he was a bleeder
Until the day he died

He started out smoking weed
Then he did a little bit of this
And a little bit of that

A little bit of heroin
And a little bit of crack

But each drug he tried
Increased his need for even greater highs
So he started selling street drugs
To pay for his jones
And stressed his mother so much
That she made him leave her home

He chose the streets
And did not even say goodbye
I can still see the tears
Streaming from his mother's eyes

Though he made triple the pay
Of the job he eventually lost
Sadly he did not know
What his lifestyle really cost

But he continued his quest
To find the ultimate high
Whatever his friends gave him
He was willing to try

He said he came alive
On his first acid trip
Said he explored the universe
Before he lost his grip

What was normal
Seemed to move so slow
And the next thing I knew
He had jumped out
A second-story window

He only broke his foot
Fate was somewhat kind

But he continued to take drugs
Until he eventually lost his mind

One day he ran outside
Bare naked in the gusting wind
He had no shame to hide
So he got thrown in a jail
With no system to really help him

He said he knew karate
That Bruce Lee was his name
And he would run back and forth
Hitting his head against the jail cell walls
Until he cried in pain

Now he walks the streets with a rag on his head
And sputters words like the living dead
He used to be funny and a master of jokes
But now the only ones laughing
Are the drug dealing folks

A Drug Story, Part II

X was a teacher
A preacher of goodwill
He used to have hopes
Of dreams fulfilled

Until X lost his mind
To dope and pills
So he walked around town
Like a man with no will

He used to be trusted
In so many ways
But when he got busted
Those closest to him had to pay

He beat his wife
Took a knife to her throat
What were hands of love
Became hands that choked
He cursed the family
That he used to protect
Now all of his children
Have lost his respect

His mother took him in
He had nowhere else to go
But he kept using heroin
And a little bit of blow

He stole from his mom
Whenever she left the house
And gave her hell
Just like he did his spouse

He never realized the deep pain
His actions brought
So he kept on stealing and drugging
Until he got caught
Now he has plenty of time
To think about how he failed
Because it has been thirteen years
Since X has been jailed

Cocaine Ain't Nothing but Pain

So you are after that gold
In that white line
You want that high
They say is better than wine

You have got the hunger
You think you are stronger
But cocaine ain't nothing but pain

You used to take pills
And sniff some glue
You have no will
And now
The white powder got you

It will mess up your mind
Have you wasting your time
And all the while you will think you are
Feeling fine

You will think you are moving fast
But you will be moving slow
Life will pass you by

And you will be the last to know
Cocaine ain't nothing but pain

You use to be worth seeing
You use to be a decent human being
But now you are acting strange
Your personality has changed
And all the time you tell me
That you are just the same

You use to have feelings
Like you really cared
But now you are into cocaine
And there is nothing there

You are giving others
What you say they need
But they stay hooked on your drugs
Just so you can succeed

So you feed their jones
Watch them destroy their homes
And you do not give up
Until they are all alone

You are making money
But you never seem to gain
Because you never have enough
To feed your own veins

So you borrow all the cash
That you can
And steal the rest
From your best friends

You think you are cool
As you pawn your stolen gold
But you are the fool you fool
Because the powder is in control
Cocaine ain't nothing but pain

You have got so good
At not telling the truth
That even you believe
What you say and do

You make pretend
And then you cry
Until even your best friends
Don't know when you lie

But your life is a mess
Though you will not confess
You just say F you
It is no one's business

But cocaine ain't nothing but pain

You can take it mixed
Or take it pure
But you will never have enough
You will always want more

It will make you wild
And make you go insane
You will have a smile
But you will be in pain

COCAINE

A Drug Story; It's Your Story Too

So many families are left behind
As we jail more people
For committing crimes
They got color TVs
And shelter from rain
It's the law to be humane

Prison cell service
Free food for those who fall
While working-class citizens pay
For those who break the law

Crimes increase with each passing day
Taxes rise to give the police more pay
Drug education to help the young
School taxes rise to supply the funds

You say you don't know anyone on dope
And that it's not your fault if they can't cope
Well
There is a drug epidemic in the land of the free
People popping pills like sweet candy
And it will not get better by letting it be

Junkies are dying, children are crying
While some of the most respected people
Are the main ones buying

Managers, engineers, operators
Everyone has to pay sooner or later
You may not know anyone
Hooked on drugs or pills
But if you don't get involved
Your taxes will be paying their bills

I SEE WHAT YOU THINK
I DON'T SEE

I See You...

I see you in the streets
And in buildings so tall
That you appear to be faceless
I see you up close and personal
A hair away from a touch

I've seen the parts of you
That you did not leave at home
I've seen the extrovert
And experienced the person
Who wants to be left all alone

I see you begging for attention
Not to mention the many ways
That you plead for your needs
Sometimes very subtle
And sometimes
Engaging in violent rebuttals

Blind eyes do not see you
Seeing eyes do not care
They do not realize
Everyone we meet

Is a reflection of
Our possibilities

So they just stare into
An empty space and hope
That you do not turn your face
In a way that your eyes
Have to recognize their presence

But I see you

Thus I laugh with you
I cry with you
I fuss with you
I have fun with you
I love you
I despise you

And I celebrate
Your life
And I celebrate
Your death

But when I interact with you
At least most of the times
I know fodder is provided
To understand myself

I see you because
You are what I was
What I am
Or what I could be

I see you when I look at me
Yes
When I look at me
I
See
You

Good Morning!

Good morning.
Good Morning?
I said Good Morning!!!

Excuse me if I irritate you with such benevolent words
I am so sorry to recognize you as a human being that is
Worthy to be recognized

Forgive me for disturbing your omnipotent being
And for being so
So irresponsibly kind
My manners just got the best of me

So please
Pardon me for not ignoring you
As you did me
I guess some of us
Just don't know any better

Dumb Smarty

You come in droves
Where you come from only heaven knows

Displaying your college degrees
Stained in alcohol and beer
You hide in the fear
That you might be discovered
And uncovered as a dumb smarty

So you move from place to place
Displacing the experience of the many
As you run the rat race
Of the good and plenty

As a matter of fact
You are on the fast track
Climbing that accelerated ladder
Where it really doesn't matter
How you get there

And in between
You hold your bladder
A little scared you might have been seen

Acting a fool at last night's party of
Dumb smartys

Future bleeders of America
You use three-hundred-pound words to hold down
Those that you know
Know more than you do

Though the purpose of communication
Is to speak in a way that others understand
Nobody knows what you are saying
Not even you
So stop acting like you know
What you say you know
Because you little twit
You really know
You don't get it
Though you are
Smart enough to act dumb about
That you do not know
What I am saying

But your greatest weakness
Other than underestimating
Those smarter than you
Is to not admit
How weak you are

And it's a shame
Because only then can you really grow
But you don't want others to know
You are just a dumb smarty

The Fake News

There is a wide array of things
That can be discussed
The earth's population is over
Seven billion six hundred
And fifty-five million plus

There are over two hundred nations worldwide
But still we accept the top three topics
The news programmers
Repeatedly provide

But fake news really thrives
Because we keep our minds
On auto drive

Topics are driven by ratings
More than the total truth
But a partial truth
Is a total lie
While too many of us
Refuse to ask why

There is nothing new
Not even the fakeness in the news
Nothing new under the sun
Just the same old story
That keeps being redone

Those in power don't want us
To see the big picture
So they feed us the news
With some Hollywood fixtures

Addictively entertained
We keep coming back
Again and again and again
And ain't nothing new
But how they manipulate our brain

Speaking fast to confuse our mind
Newscasters cut off the experts
And leave the truth behind

It's a war of words
They refuse to surrender
Because each station has
Their own agenda

As ratings soar
They exploit the rich
But more so the poor

And they fool the weak
And they fool the wise
As the truth we all seek
Gets sensationalized

Their research shows
It really doesn't matter to most of us
So they know
How to take a simple thing
And make it fatter to increase
Our interest and trust

That which is small and contrite
Gets blown out of proportion
Exciting the viewers to commit
Intellectual abortion
As we get so stressed
That we can't sleep at night

Then there's the fake news
Propagated by the politicians
Whose main goal is to keep us
In a subservient condition

Lies come from the Left
And lies come from the Right
Each one claiming
They have seen the light

But as we watch the fake news
Designed just for us
Agreeing with the Left or Right
Is an absolute must

We argue with each other
About what is true
And gather together
Only with those who agree
With our biased views

But the things we say about others
Can be so mean
Especially the things we say
Behind the scenes

You see
We the people
Can be more fake
Than anything
On the fake news

But without hesitation
We always say it's more fake
On the other news station

But when we watch
Our favorite program

We see only
What we want to see

Then slowly but surely
We become
Fake people programmed
By the fake news
That we are programmed to watch
On our favorite programmed TV

Indentured Servants

Are we meant to exist
Without the right kind of pay
Programmed to buy things that don't add value
But take all of our money away
Only to get a long-term loan
That has us paying
Twice the value of our home

Programmed to save money in a bank
We receive a profit of less than two percent
While the bank takes our money
And makes a three hundred percent profit
From our dead presidents

Most employers don't pay us
An honest day's check
They just pay us enough
To keep honest people in check
So we work all our lives
But never seem to get ahead
If we let them
They will own everything but our hurt
Until the day we are dead

It's an endless battle we fight
As we spend more than we can save
While we put more money
In the other guys' pockets
Then give him our last few dollars
To bury us in our grave

So are we truly free
Or just indentured servants
Disguised as middle class
Want to be's

We are pitted against each other
To get a few more crumbs
If we banded together
There would be more than enough
For everyone

But we work and we work
To make another man rich
And receive so little
That we feel like his bitch

But we get just enough
To soften our hurt
As the rich get richer
Off of our hard work

We seek a freedom
That seems so distant
And the more we try
The more we can't
Because we
Have been programmed
All of our lives
To be the rich man's
Indentured servant

Beneath Their Tears

Man's inhumanity to man
Causes a wrenching in my spirit
A tear in my emotional fabric
That bears a pain that lies
Beneath their tears

And in a shame for humanity
I cry when no one can hear
For laughter has replaced the respect
That people used to have
When tears fell from men in pain

But now the best that you can expect
Is the only one most people care about
Is
No one

With pride they celebrate
The class destruction of sanity
Which enables them to use
Weapons of mass destruction
To destroy humanity

And then
They spend their time blaming each other
But the bottom line is
It is they who are killing
Their sisters and brothers

They point fingers that stretch across
Culture nations and continents
And use unjustifiable warfare
To slaughter the innocent

They even agree on how to kill
Then make peace treaties
That they know
They will not fulfill

They claim and they blame
But it's all the same
They do not really care
Because there is no shame
Hidden beneath their tears

So they continue
To kill to prevent killing
And then they kill and kill
And kill again ad-infinium

In their quest to end their wars quickly
They use weapons of mass destruction

And obliterate any evidence
Of their obstruction of justice

But their greatest weapon you see
Is the psychological warfare
Created to obstruct the truth
And control the masses
As they gaslight them
Into alternate realities
Used to perpetrate their muse
And create leeches
In a game hidden by fake tears
And prepared speeches

It is a thrilling adventure for some
Because they don't know or understand
There is nothing but eternal death
When their day is done

They control the old the young
The helpless and the poor
And fill their pockets
As they brainwash others
To do their chores

They have no heart
And they have no fear
Their eyes are dry

Because there is no love
Beneath their tears

Millions of their outer selves are destroyed
Because of their insensitivity
As the war of their inner selves
Destroys the great human they could be

But when they destroy others
They destroy a piece of themselves
And the hell they create on earth
In their endless quest for wealth
Puts our very survival at stake
But one day soon
Their arrogant smile
Will be wiped off their face

They will look for fame
But there will be no applause
Only silence surrounded by fear
And as they fight their lost cause
There will be no compassion
Beneath our tears

They will regret without change
And laugh without joy
But they will be in pain
And their souls destroyed

Their closed eyes will not rest
As they will open and stare
Then maybe
Sadness will finally flow
Hidden deep
Beneath their tears

Enemy of The State

Yes
I
Am
Smart
And the only classification of intelligence
That I assign to myself
My family and my friends
And I really mean this
Is that of genius

Because it is the only intelligence category
That has no limits for upper intellectual growth
And the only category that I define
My capacity to learn and know

All other categories
Designed by the super wealthy
Are designed to control
So that they can keep
All the wealth they stole
From those who sleep

The elite fear most
Those who are awake
They and their servants
Call themselves Patriots
And we
The Enemy of the State

I see the rich and powerful
Hiding behind big red ties
And when they run out of camouflage
They hide behind their lies

Yes
I am an enemy of the state
I know that those in power
Want to keep the rest of us poor
In bad health and divided
As the cost of living soars
That way they can have even more
As we stand around undecided
Waiting for them to tell us
What to do who we are
And what to live for

The controlled minds
Accept the paradigms
That we have limited time
Based on their stats

But this is predicated on the fact
That if we continue to take in
Their contaminated
Water and air
Eat their artery-coating
Meats oils and cheese
Then we will die according to
Their projected life expectancies

But not me
I have decontaminated my mind
Left all the lies and myths far behind
I have found a better way to live
Far beyond their statistical fallacies
I am spoiled and defined by a God
Who truly loves me

I have learned to discern
That which is real
From that which is fake
Therefore
I am the enemy of the state

I reject a nationalism
That denies a connection
And an affection for all
I deny the insanity
That denies humanity

A world where power
Wealth and prosperity
Has been forcefully taken
By the rich and greedy
From the many who are poor and needy

But I am not on the run
There is too much at stake
So I am asking you to join me
As enemy of the state

I SEE YOUR HURT

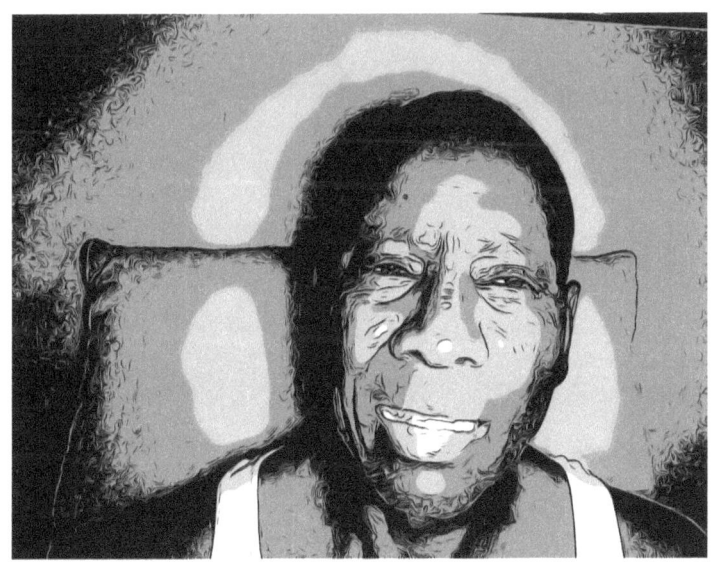

I Wish

I wish the world was different
I dream of a better time
I know there must be cloudy days
But I still miss the sunshine

I wish that families would stay together
But they pull apart because they will not bend
Stretched too far are broken hearts
So women live without their men

Children suffer while mothers cry
Fathers run when they hurt inside
It seems they do not know what to do
When love and pain collide

I wish that you could love me more
Just like I love you
Touch me with more compassion
And do what lovers do

I wish the sun was shining bright
But it's a cold and cloudy day

I wish that you could hold me tight
When I feel you slip away

I wish that you were kinder
And loved me unrestrained
I wish that I could find the strength
To love you just the same

Then maybe the world could see
True love
Through you and me

I wish!

Lost and Never Found

I looked into his face
But did not see the grace
That God had given me
The hope I found
He had long forgotten
Hope not to mention ever again

He had a spontaneous laugh
Caused by memories of where he'd been
His face was worn-torn
And defeated from within
Only he and God knows
All the despicable places he's been

He told me a story
Of a life lost and never found
Trying to find higher ground
Away from the flood of problems
That wore his soul down

He had laid sprayed and made kids
But was never a father
He never bothered

Never had time
Too busy trying to get a dime of this
And a dime of that
And no time to raise what he called
His ghetto brats
He didn't even know he
Made them like that

As a matter of fact
When I told him I raised all my kids
He thought I was kidding
He even said I was lying
Cause he ain't seen his kids in fifteen years
And he ain't even trying

But he's trying to forget where he's been
Though he knows not where he is at
But he likes it like that

He is a marginal man
Half man and half illusion
Can't take a stand
Because he is full of confusion

He talks about how the man
Keeps holding him down
But he is the man
That he has never found

The Investment

(A letter to the anonymously hurt)

You have invested all these years living in fear
Holding onto a love that keeps you in tears
I know your heart wants to be committed
But your body can not forget it
Forget that is
All the hurt and pain caused by
The love you invested without gain

Stained with dreams not realized
You scream like someone has died
You know time is not on your side
But still you invest in him
As if you can change him

Because you don't know how to quit
Though you cannot forget
How happy you used to be
Before you met your greatest source of misery
But still you invest in the devil
Because he has the fire

And you hide your burns
Underneath your attire

Though expensive clothes cannot hide
The many scars on your thighs
And the scars still show beneath
Fancy dark sunglasses
That fail to hide your swollen eyes
Or the tears that you cry

Sadly you still know
What no one knows
He tries to hide your bruises
By hitting you beneath your clothes

Even so you listen to his lies
False truths told and scolded
And hailed at you
Impaling your emotions like spears
That pierce your confidence
And devotion with fear
Again and again and again
But not enough to leave him

Like pouring money into a car
That is nothing but a lemon
You ride out the dents and scars
Because you hate to waste
All the love you have given

You pour love into him
Just like gas wasted
Driving around in circles
In an endless loop that always ends
Where it begins
Nowhere
But still you embrace it

You have convinced yourself
That you have invested too much
To allow someone else to feel his touch
A touch that you know is only warm
When he wants something
That you can no longer give

What used to make you feel
Erotically alive
Has died long before he realized
It was gone

You need to slow down your pace
And make an assessment
Of your ill-made investment
A decision you made in haste
An investment of emotions overdone
With a net return of one minus one

Sincerely, I See You

Lost in The Mirror

She gets lost in the mirror
And cannot see herself
She comes nearer and nearer
But she sees someone else

She puts makeup on her face
And dreams she is a movie star
It is a self-made tragedy
Where she hides her childhood scars

A little bit of skin cream
To brighten her complexion
Though her mind is in the dark
Without much direction

She really is a queen
But she does not recognize
That she is lost in the mirror
With blinders around her eyes

A beautiful woman
Hiding behind a dream

Lost in the mirror
Where all is not what it seems

She puts contacts in her eyes
To turn them ocean blue
What a shame she does not know
Her brown eyes are so beautiful

Then she straightens her hair
Until it slowly falls out
But even her long blond wig
Cannot erase her doubt

She had hair like the queens
Traced back to Africa
With skin so dark and lovely
Not needing any makeup

But now she is in a movie
Casted as a star and a fan
Lost in a mirror
Trying to do the best she can

All I Got Is My Walk

I don't have a job
No place to call my own
Only pennies from a government
That wants to control me with a loan

Sometimes I feel like
I'm on a rendezvous with death
You see
I ain't got nothing left
But my walk

It's a Black man's walk
Tilted to the side
Like an ankle is broke
But you know who I am
By the swag of my stroke

I swing my arms
And create my space
I walk so cool
It will make you feel out of place

I command the sidewalk
As strangers scurry to the street
They're the same grey suits
Who use to boss me
But I feel like a giant
At five foot three

With a little bit of attitude
And a long smooth stride
All my problems
Become easy to hide

Faded shirts and holes in my shoes
Nothing of worth and not much to do

So the mean streets
Are my curse to roam
My only other choice
Is the hot attic where I sleep
In someone else's home

But no matter how much I hurt
It is my walk
That makes me feel like I have
Something of worth

There's a beat in my walk
That matches the street in my talk

I was briefly college educated
Dropped out eight years ago

Lord knows I should have waited
Perhaps
If I tried a little harder
I could have graduated

But still I can talk
A little bit of uppity smack
But my walk stays the same
Because I
Like it like that

I step to a different rhythm
And a different rhyme
No dollars in my pockets
Only nickels and dimes

That gives me a quarter note beat
Perfect in time
And I feel good inside
Because my walk is all mine

Just jingle in my pockets
Just like I said
So I lengthen my stride
And bobble my head

No dead presidents
Everything I make
Is already spent
But I have a walk
That will make you
Want to pay all my rent

There's no shine on my shoes
Just holes in my sole
I feel the morning dew
On feet as black as coal

But I move with a swagger
As sharp as a dagger
That matches the street in my talk

It's an intoxicated sophistication
You see
All I got is my walk.

Stinky Don't Know

Stinky thinks he is cool
But Stinky don't know
Stinky just stinks from head to toe

Just got high from smoking crack
Stinky got a smell that will knock you back
But Stinky don't care
That he smells like sin

He just smiles a silly smile
And says
Hey cuz where you been

Stinky wants to play
But he stinks so bad
It will make a skunk
Run away mad

He be sweating and thinking
And thinking and stinking
And when he opens his mouth
It will have your eyes blinking
He got a stink so thick

That you will hope
That his odor will not stick

I gave him a suit
So he could go to church
But Stinky did not know
What good clothes are worth

He just threw it on the floor
In the corner of his room
And my fine suit collected dust and dirt
Cause Stinky don't use a broom

Then he put on a shirt
That had more wrinkles than his face
And when I asked him why
He just said
Let's get out of this funky place

So I said come on Stinky
Let's take a ride into town
But he stank so much
I had to turn around

I said Stinky
Why are you going like this
Your clothes are dirty
And you smell like cat piss

It was a stench so bad
That I found it hard to bear
And after he left
It smelled like he was still there

So I aired out my car
For three whole days
Lit incense and even sprayed
But even then
The smell still stayed

The next time I seen Stinky
It was at a family affair
And Stinky had a smell
Like abused underwear

He was standing in a corner
Drinking some cheap gin
And the smell got worse
As I approached him

I was hoping for the best
Like maybe it wasn't Stinky
Perhaps it was a skunk
But the closer I got
I knew it had to be Stinky's funk

And just as bad
Was the stench coming from his mouth

It stank so bad
He should have never left his house
He said hey cuz where you been
It was like he didn't even know
He smelled like dead skin

He was wearing lopsided sunglasses
With his hat tipped to the side
And an outdated shirt
That smelled like it needed to be washed
With three boxes of Tide®

A closer look at Stinky's shirt
Revealed that it was inside out
But when I told Stinky
He said with much pride
I know I am wearing it this way
But it's faded on the opposite side

Yes his shirt was inside out
Because the other side was faded
But Stinky didn't care
Because his thoughts were so jaded

Even so I checked up on Stinky again
What am I supposed to do
He is one of my best friends
Even if he smells like an old shoe

On his step were three young women
Two looked like the walking dead
And going nowhere
The other not looking too bad
But looked like
She was not supposed to be there

And when I asked them
Where is Stinky
In unison they spoke

Stinky is really cool
But he has a smell that ain't no joke

We like Stinky
That is a fact
But we be sitting out here
Because we had enough of his smell
But Stinky don't know that

I told them to tell Stinky
That I said hello
Because I got a whiff of Stinky's room
And said hell I got to go

Several times I have told Stinky
He needs to wash more
But every time I told him

He just said come on cuz
Take me to the liquor store

It's a sad story and that's a fact
But Stinky don't care
Because Stinky don't know that

Stinky thinks he is cool
But Stinky don't know
Stinky just stinks
From his hair
To his crusty toe

DO YOU SEE
WHAT I SEE?

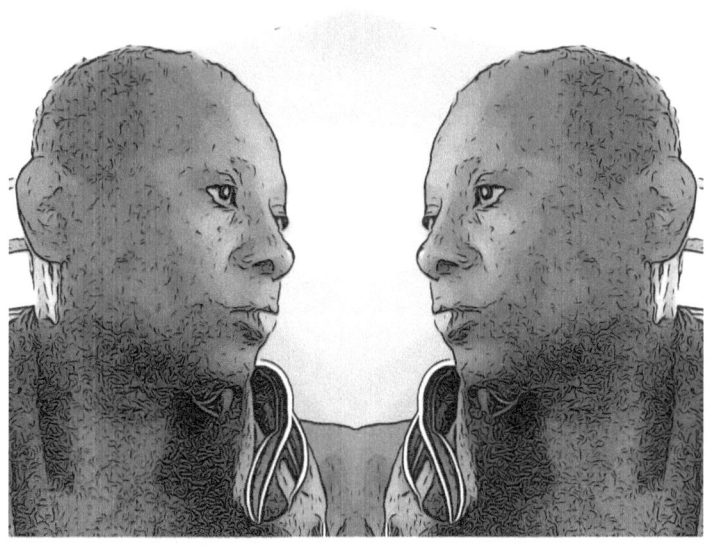

They Is Us

We are the ones who like to fuss
Point fingers at them and say
It is them not us
They did this and they did that
And
They are the ones who killed the cat

Those people are so ignorant
That it makes me sick
If I were them I would have never
Done that or this

The world is screwed and so messed up
But they are the blame
It's going down and not up
Because when I do the same
At least I know when
Enough is enough

How could they have elected him
The world would be better
If they elected the other has been

I know they are hurting
But those people are just so dumb
They did not realize
We were just having fun

Why judge me for what they did
They might be my ancestors
Who did all that past shit
But who cares
If they paved the way
For the privileges I get
Can't you see
That was them and this is me
They are the ones who wrote history

When you point your fingers at others
Three come back to you
But we are always blaming they
For the things we do

And every major race and culture
Has committed great atrocities
It's easy to see if you look at all of history

So in true reflection I must say
The people that we say are they
Are just a projection of the things
I

You
Me
We
Do
And say

Niggers, Coloreds and the Man

Niggers are always going around saying
That's my nigger
Because they have falsely figured
That they have changed the word nigger to something good
But the only people who have accepted that distorted fact
Are niggers

It is rejected by everyone else
Because they still think
A nigger is a nigger
Is a nigger

You see
A nigger will walk around
With his pants hanging down
Looking like happy the clown
And not even realize
He is the laughing stock of the town
He can't get a job
But don't know why
So he will rob and steal
And punch you in the eye

With his pants hanging all over his shoes
He will look you in the face
And without disgrace say
What else could I do

You see
Niggers love to steal
They steal and steal and steal
And then steal some more
Just for the thrill of it

And then
They will try to make you feel like
It is your fault
Knowing they ain't got nothing
That they ever bought
They feel quite comfortable
Stealing from you the possessions
You have worked a lifetime to obtain
Because your pain does not matter to a nigger

You see
The nigger national anthem is
Your pain is my gain
Easy money the easy way
Niggers love to rob you
Of your hard-earned pay

And niggers like to party
Niggers will party
All night long
Niggers will party
Until their arms are stinky stank strong

And niggers will take a birdbath in a minute
Be out of the water before they are in it
And then they will use some cheap deodorant
And not even realize
They still got that awful scent

But still they will party on
And turn up the music
Until the break of dawn

Niggers love to play loud obnoxious music
They don't care that nobody else wants to hear it
But niggers will stand up and go crazy
For rapping that be slapping
Their brothers and sisters down
Then turn up their music louder
When more niggers come around

And as the volume goes higher and higher
Like a town crier
They will proudly yell out
That's my nigger

Because they can't figure
A nigger is a nigger is a nigger
But when they are questioned by the man
For using the word nigger
They say you just don't understand
You be in the fog
Because that nigger over there
That's my dog

But there's more to being a nigger
Than the friendly coin they try to spend
Much about being a nigger
Is playing make pretend

They be dressing like clowns
With pierced skin and tattoos
All up and down

They wear symbols
They don't understand
But they don't care
As long as they look different from the man
Then they go for a job looking like a has been
And wonder why the man won't let them in
And niggers always seem to have an itch
To call their woman a bitch
Got some of their women
Even liking it

But I know that's not you
That's just what niggers do

And then there's colored folks
They joke back and forth
About how the man did this
And the man did that

Don't they understand
Any man will only do to you
What you allow them to do to you

And by the way
Why can't coloreds
Be the man

If they, coloreds that is
Ain't the man
Then what are they
Boys?
You see
Hidden in their smiles
Coloreds receive a certain amount of joy
Of being juvenile

As they smile and laugh and joke
At not having the responsibilities
That a real man has
They poke fun at their sisters and brothers

Then put the man up on a stand
That even he cannot command

Because in reality
The man is just as messed up
As the coloreds
They just know how to grandstand
Better than the darker fellows

But coloreds like to put on a show
Just for the man
They will "Yasser" their boss all day
For two more cents an hour
And give the boss all the power
That could be theirs to command

Instead of miming
Everybody else's business
They could be masters
Of their own land

But they don't realize
They could own their own business
Even when their boss
Is less skilled and knowledgeable
Than them
You see
It's not that the man really is superior

It's just that he has managed
To convince the coloreds
That they are inferior

So coloreds go around calling each other
Stupid and dumb
And walk around with their pants on the ground
Like they are some kind of bum
Listed in the lost and not found

And when they run out of names to call each other
They just say
That's my nigger

But coloreds work hard for their money
Then buy large screen TVs,
Gold jewelry
And plenty of fancy clothes

Anything that depreciates
Because they don't appreciate
The power
Of money

And everyone knows
They will rent before they buy
And spend, spend, spend
To create wealth for the other guy

The other guy being of course
The man

And every two or three years
Coloreds are sure to buy a fancy car
So that they may be on display
Just to have a nigger
Come and take it all away

While the man just sits back and laughs
Because he knows he's going to get his pay
You see the pawn shops are full of coloreds
Trying to give their money away to
You guessed it
The man

Coloreds bend over backward
Allowing the man to stand tall
On an unlevel plane
And stand on them for his own gain

The man even got coloreds
Trained to prey upon each other
That's P-R-E-Y not P-R-A-Y
Sounds like
Some kind of Willie Lynch kind of shit
Doesn't it

Trained like crabs in a pan
They hold each other down
From making a stand
Giving all power
To
The man

Most do nothing
About their substandard living conditions
But go around saying
The man is always holding us down

And in their illusion and confusion
They say the only one who takes good care of me
Is
My nigger

He got the best drugs
And liquor galore
And when he runs out
He will spend his last dollar
To get some more

But coloreds think they are better than niggers
Because somehow they figure
The man will hire them
To keep niggers in check
But

Niggers and coloreds actually created the man
They gave him the platform for which he stands

But at the end of the day
The man doesn't give either one
Any respect

After all is said and done
Both are the blame
You see the man looks at niggers and coloreds
As one and the same!

Twilight Zone USA

There is a fifth dementia
Beyond that which we understand
A middle ground between right
And the ridiculous
Denying science for stupid-diction
It lies between the trick of man's fears
And the summit of his gullibility
This is the dementia of a lost nation
That has lost its way
In an area we call
Twilight Zone USA

It was a time when the popular vote
Gave way to the electoral
And the will of the majority
Was suppressed without a memorial

A polling miscalculation
Missed by the intellectuals
A misrepresentation
Of the power of the super rich
When the data-don't-lie
Became twilight zone ineffectual

So I cried when a fool was elected
An orange-faced narcissist obsessed with red ties
Who hoped his stupidity would not be detected
If he told enough lies
He sent a nation
Into a dysfunctional state
Because his state of mind
Was dysfunctional

He was a great big bully
Full of bull manure
A man-child who never fully matured
A billionaire just like Warren Buffet
But he was always running scared
Because he was nothing but a puppet
And a true paragon
Of a political moron

The biggest threat was not
This wannabe king
It was those who had the real power
Who made him sing
They needed him to pass
Laws that were absurd
And they knew he would sign them
Without reading the words

So they stroked his ego
Like he was a little kid

But hid behind his back
And laughed at the stupid things
He said and did

They had no desire to console him
But they needed to keep him in the
School of fools to control him

So they gave him a big red tie
And informed him red stands for power
But they purposely did not tell him
That it would lose its potency
If he wore it every hour

He was so obsessed
With being the only one admired
His red tie became the main piece
Of his want-to-look-important attire

On rare occasions
He would wear a blue tie
A color his controllers told him
Represents trust
But he told so many lies
It made the people cuss

He was convinced he could stealth his lies
Whenever he wore his blinding red ties
And anyone questioning his judgment

Found their career ready to expire
So they agreed with the fake king
Who was nothing but a pathological liar

He got a slick weave in his aging hair
For this man-child was obsessed
With his outward appearance
But it made him look like a patient
Leaving a mental hospital without any clearance

But still the people fed his ego
And let him have his way
Becoming a part of the stupid-diction
In the Twilight Zone USA

Unknown to him his big red tie
Could not make this simpleton
Seem like he was strong
His own people wrote books
Of how he did things wrong

He lied so much every day
That he was the biggest cause
Of trumping credibility
In the Twilight Zone USA

Sometimes he opened his jacket
And strutted across
The middle-ground white lawn

A sign that many lies would be told
From dusk until dawn

His staff cringed
When he did not use his teleprompter
Because they knew he would be on
An endless lying binge
That they would be ashamed to sponsor

When his incompetence got exposed
He would find someone else to blame
Because the only thing he cared about
Was his political campaign

It got so bad
That his dedicated groupie base
Used alternate realities to explain
How the truth can be replaced

Afraid to be bullied
If they did not support his lies
His base stood by his side
Wearing their own red ties
A madness exploited
And blatantly undignified

Twilight Zone USA
A plutocracy masqueraded as a democracy

A hypocrisy that used alternate realities
To explain the actions
Of an emotionally stunted fool
That committed moral and ethical infidelity

The rich got richer
The poor made more poor
And the greedy agenda of the wealthy
Gave them even more

There was no retribution
As the right to vote them out
Became harder to restore
Because they ignored their constitution
And stole even more

But let us get back to the bleeder
In this twilight tale
The incompetent leader
Who had terrible secrets
That could land him in jail
Like his corrupt tax return
That made him look like a gangster
Headed for a long jail term

A stable genius
Is the name he gave himself
Person woman man camera TV

Words weaklings repeat
When they have poor mental health

Even those closest to him who claimed
They would always have his back
Knew he was just a Con
Away from alternative facts

He was a fool who denied science
For his personal political stand
And many unnecessarily suffered
When a virus spread across the land
As he blundered the many resources
That were under his command

Even he got sick from the virus
And many close to him got sick as well
Just like a pied piper tyrant
Leading slaves straight to hell

Still his people hoped that one day
He would act like someone
Who could take the country back to
The make America hate again old ways

But a president can act like a fool
Though a fool can't act like a president
For you can fool some of the people

Some of the time
But you can't fool all of the people
When you cannot stop lying

Thus is the dementia of a nation
That has lost its way
Such is the plight of life
In the Twilight Zone USA

The Patriots

Some of the self-proclaimed patriots
Of the so-called United States
Were born of fear
Isolated from diversity
And brain-stained to hate

They have an orange-faced leader
They worship day and night
Because he convinces them
Their evil ways are right
There are very good people on both sides he says
Even when one side desires the other
To be their forever slaves

I'm not talking about our brave soldiers
And other real Patriots
I'm talking about the want-to-be masters
And the unamerican Hitler type bigots

They go around dragging flags
Throughout the nation
You see them on pickup trucks
Cars and front porches and
Southern gas stations

For they adore and worship their flag
As much as their orange-faced abomination

Afraid they will reap what they have sown
Before they enter perdition
They run from their sins of yesterday
Because there is no contrition
For their evil ways

These are the self-proclaimed patriots
Known by their MAGA® hats
And confederate flags
They idolize statues that represent
A past they wish they still had

Make American great again they say
But only the privileged patriots
Want a return to a time
When people were forced to work
Without being payed

patriots
They stand on the shoulders of their ancestors
Who stole just about everything they got
Stole the land from the Indian and Mexican
Stole labor and freedom from the African-American
Stole the wages from the Chinese
Who they forced to build railroads
Across the patriots stolen land

They stole in the name of
Manifest destiny and gentrification
Legalities formed to suppress others
In their institutionalized racist greedy nation

They worship stone-cold memorials
Of those who betrayed the USA
But patriots don't care because
They long for yesterday

They proudly flash their cards from the NRA®
And talk about how the second amendment
Is slowly slipping away
So they buy more and more guns
And plenty of ammunition
And form militias
To protect their past traditions

They walk around carrying tiki torches
Singing Jews will never replace us
Acting like scared little grown up kids
Trained to be racist
A herd mentality
That has committed many historical brutalities

Trying to turn peaceful protests
Into moments of terror
They infiltrate the movement for justice

So they can make it seem like an error

patriots they say
But what they do
Is truly not the American way
How can they proclaim
Truth and justice for all
And at the same time shout
Build that wall
Pay their Mexican laborers
Substandard wages
While they put their children
In iron cages

patriots hate anything
Other than a reflection of them
And they have conditioned those that they hate
To assimilate without having all the rights
And protection of the United States

So forgive me if I don't call myself a patriot
Not the way the word has been morphed
Because today's patriot is code for
Racism has been endorsed

It is a madness affecting reason
And it is as dangerous
As treason

Racism Is A Cult

Racism is a cult
Ignorance easily brought
Paid with prejudice
That is purposely taught
To control the minds of the distraught

Racism is one of the greatest sins
A denial of the human family
Based on the color of one's skin
And the mass hysteria
That others are inferior

Racism replaces intellect with insanity
Depriving the rationale of equality
It is an insecurity of minorities
A separator of humanity
Steeped deep in moral infidelity
Self-hate and personal insecurities

Racism is a cult
Wrought with philosophical imperfections
Creating a deception of perception
That stealths the evil connection

Of those who are privileged
As they brainwash others
To follow their self-serving obsessions

They pillage the underclass
And amass great wealth
Then deny from all others
Their finances
Safety and health

Suppressing all pleasantries
Words are weaponized
To create feelings of inferiority
Many names are manufactured
To abuse minorities
But one of the worst names used
Being black nigger

But they are truly
The niggers they figured
Are those who are dark
For they project unto them
The awful people
They
Really are

This racist cult is designed
To usher urban peasantry
Into generational poverty

Thus racists use law and injustice
Not meant for them
But designed to bust just us
Or anything considered leftwing
Into social-cultural-financial phlegm
Expectorated as
Casualties of cultural cleansing

But in their effort to suppress others
And create the illusion that all others
Are inferior to them
It is the cult that harbors
The wildest animals in the land
Creating a paradox
They will never understand
Because it is their racist acts
That make them less of a man

They attack in superior numbers
Because most are afraid to fight
One on one
That's why these cowards
Hide behind hoods
And carry guns

Racists live in such fear
That they amass
Massive arsenals of weapons

Weapons that were originally meant
For the military
But it is their immense insecurities
That really make them scary

For they worry that in the very hour
That they lose their power and worth
They will be devoured by those
To which they have unleashed
Unending and inhuman atrocities
On every continent on the earth

This cult of the underdeveloped
Cannot imagine
That those they suppress and torture
Are capable of forgiving them
Of their centuries-old sins
And how they have always acted
Like scared barbarians

So they discriminate against others
And teach their children
That's the way it's always been
Therefore the cult is maintained
From the hate grown from within
And nurtured by
Ignorance and pain

Racists define the truth
From an imaginary place
Sisterhood and brotherhood
Are defaced
Making love thy brother and sister
As thyself
Seem intellectually
Out of place

Swastikas are used to signify
They are better
Than the ones they despise
And they will suppress
Kill and torture
Those who think otherwise

But even skin plastered
With symbolic tattoos
Cannot make men out of children
Who know not what they do

Racism makes about as much sense
As superman thinking
That putting on glasses
Disguises him as Clark Kent

But some racists substitute glasses
With white hoods

Cowards afraid to be exposed
As the no good they really represent

The members of this bastard-minded cult
Claim they are the master race
A ridiculous premise
That makes a very weak case
And accepted by the insecure
And easily convinced
It uses a narrow set of knowledge
To narrow the minds
Of those who refuse
To look for real evidence

Even when presented with data
Based on science and fact
They hold on to mythologies
Like a junkie hooked on crack

Their heroes include slave hoarders
Rapists and psychopaths
But it is a cult formed to create servants
To control wealth for the upper class

Racism is a cult that worships leaders
That lack moral and ethical devotion
Users who train losers
And other castrated intellects

To sink into a quicksand of
Their many issues and emotions
The cult is populated with fools
That fight to end civil rights
And defend their heroes' statues and symbols
Rather than defend
The taking of innocent human life

Eight minutes and forty-six seconds
Of televised murder
That most civil people condemned
Because law and justice were sacrificed
Meant nothing to them
Because none of their own
Had to pay the ultimate price

Though the greatest commandment is
Love thy neighbor as thyself
Racists rather believe
Their foolish cult doctrines
That promote they are superior
To everyone else

While their cult abhors
Treating everyone nice
They worship fiery crosses
But deny the cross of Christ

They are the confused that refuse
To accept their own issues
And continue to press down on those
Different than them

Then they build walls
Cage innocent children
And spend Sunday morning in church
Hollering and screaming
Amen
While the rest of us know
They are nothing but fake Christians

Though Jesus Christ
Died on a cross to deny hatred
Using his life to usher love through
Racists hide behind their rituals
Continue to burn a cross or two
And commit crimes against humanity
Then write books of history
That hide the truth of their inhumanity

And with hateful pride they dehumanize
Those they colonize and terrorize
So they can rationalize and justify
The different cultures they cannibalize

They are a cult full of psychopaths
That laugh at the suffering of the outcast
Narcissists who twist the truth
To make their false legacy last

Racists commit unambiguous
Hideous acts
And then make insidious
Retractions of the facts

But their hateful oppressions of others
Will create a cult in hell
For all of them to exist
Forever and indiscriminately trapped
In a vault full of burning crosses
Strung together with their fellow racists

Five-Fifths of a Human Being

I am five-fifths of a human being
Two more fifths than what you are seeing
I said five-fifths
I am total and complete
And I refuse to accept your definition
Of what I am supposed to be

You see my darkness
But refuse to see my light
You see my difference
As an excuse not to treat me right

You might think you and yours are the best
But mine and me are just as good
And nothing less

Can't you count
One two three four five
Or are you so ignorant
That you cannot count that high

Stop using your maniac math
To judge me

And your prejudiced eyes
To judge
Only what you want to see
And all that you despise

And stop gauging my IQ
Or how slow I do the things that I do
I have the right to make mistakes
Just like you

You are not the standard by any means
And who told you that you have perfect genes
It ain't nothing but your immaturity
That you project onto others
Because of your own insecurity

You have tried to make me less
By denying my right to vote and read
But still I passed every test
I was built to succeed

Though you tried hard
To change my course
I overcame every obstacle
Even when under-resourced
It was I that made you sweat
Like a dripping popsicle

So look at me
I have risen from
Your unequal playing fields
And generations of slavery

Kings and Queens
Held against their will
But still we rose
From every cotton field
Even if you do not see it
Because you are so conceited
I am whole
And I am God-completed

From my hair to my feet
Everything you are seeing
Is five-fifths
Five-fifths
Of a human being

REVELATIONS

Everybody Has Their Time

Everybody has their time
Their time and space
A place in time to be somebody
Somebody special
Especially made for
Their time
And
Their space

What you do with your time
Is your choice
But what you choose
Determines if you regret or rejoice
Win or lose

A grave dug with dreams unfulfilled
And gifts not manifested
Can never justify the thrill
Of a life filled with dreams
 Uncontested

Time can go fast
Or time can go slow

How you spend your time
Determines how fast it goes

If you spend your time complaining
And abstaining from the things
That you should do
Then time will go as slow
As a turtle
Walking on glue

But if you are the answer
And a person that spreads
Love and joy
You can overcome
The demon cancer
That thief in the night
That comes only to destroy

Though your time
May seem to go fast
You will reap the reward
Of time that forever will last

Your time
Has a Divine assignment
An assignment
Just for you
Between birth and death
It matters what you do

You can leave a footprint
Formed from disunity
Hatred and hurt
Or a legacy
That unites and nurtures
All living beings
On this great planet earth

May your time be filled
With acts of kindness
That outshines the darkness
That enslaves the mindless

Bear in mind
It is your duty
To reach out to
All of humankind

Be better caretakers
Of everyone
And all of life
For we are all intertwined

We live on this earthly timeshare
Here today but at any moment
Our time on earth can go away
Like a mist in the air
Never here to stay

That does not make us strong
Nor does it make us weak
But everybody has their time and space
And that makes us truly unique

So spend your time wisely
For time is a gift
A gift of exceptional value
A gift that can never be replaced

And always remember
How much time you have
Is determined by how you live
And God's mercy and grace

Why I Don't Cry at Funerals

People wonder why I don't cry at funerals
They question my love
As if love can be encapsulated in a tear
Not knowing the dew coming from their eyes
Is a result of the things they didn't do
For the ones they said they loved so dearly

Their guilt overflows from a heart
That could not drive their body
To do the things of love

Rather their actions were spent on
Loving the things they do
And
Forgetting the ones they say they loved

Even now they think of themselves
Thinking they will miss their loved ones
More than their loved ones will miss heaven

They come to funerals ready to cry
And fan away the sweat of their anxiety

And stare at motionless bodies
That lie in expensive throw-away beds of pine

Hoping their tears will relieve them of their grief
They think of memories that could have been
But never were because they were too busy
Never having time for the living
But always having time for the dead

They cry and they cry and they cry some more
Trying to ignore the things they could have done
For the newly deceased
They look at me and wonder
Why don't I cry at funerals?

So on rare occasions
I'll answer them
Unrestrained
I don't cry at funerals because
I give the living sunshine instead of rain

The Beginning of Wisdom

The Holy Bible says
Fear of the Lord is the beginning of wisdom
But people do not fear
For they have become too dumb to hear

The voice of God

They hear only the selfish voice
Of their own pride
So they hide
From the fear of their self

Help is on the way they say
So they pop pills
Trying to regain the thrill of yesterday
Or they pay one hundred dollars an hour
For others to listen to the story of
How they lost their power

They holler like a child
That does not know how to stop crying
And continue lying to themselves
Refusing to acknowledge

That the only true help
Is in the Lord

But they do not fear the Lord

So children try to act like grown-ups
And grown-ups act like childish children

They horde more and more of their addictions
Addictions that come in many forms
Drugs, adultery, lying stealing,
And many more become their new norms

Reeling from the pain within
They hurt others again and again
Because they don't realize
The root of all addictions is sin
It is an affliction of humankind
It is the reason why
Many will be left behind

People think they know
But they don't know
The Creator
The Lord our God
Is where all truth comes from

But they run towards sin
And away from Him
Because they don't know
Fear
Of the Lord
Is the beginning of wisdom

The Children of Mankind

Lord let there be green in this barren land
The crust can't feed all the children of man
The air is thick and harmful to breathe
The skies made of poisonous fog from our greed

May our heart change let it beat anew
It is time to be responsible for the things we do
The children of mankind need a brand new start
We can make a change once we change our heart

We should stand tall against hate and sin
Instead we build walls that lock us in
If we can't change when we hurt ourselves
How can we change if we hurt someone else?

The children of mankind are tired of our vanity
We have got to change to save humanity
The animal life and plant life scream from their girth
And beg us to take better care of the earth

We reject love and abuse our environment
And leave very little hope for our descendants

But a present made of rejection
Will give us a future without protection

For the earth's and heaven's sake
There is so much more at stake
Than just our own likeness
All of life is affected by our mess

So let us pledge a new covenant
To be much more prudent with our environment
And no longer drunk with emotional moonshine
And take better care of the planet for
The children of mankind

The Virus

It started centuries ago
Causing humans to go
Indiscriminately insane
Surviving like vampires choking
Every drop of sanity out of our brains

Gaining ground as the killing increased
It started as the smallest thing on earth
A thought turned into insanity
Manifested into horrible actions
Justified as necessary progress
For a civilized humanity

As the thoughts increased
And got more scary
So did the deceased
So much that some were left unburied

As it took over its host
The virus grew strong
Enflaming the land
Like burnt toast

Killing and feeding upon itself
It multiplied and spread
The human host prayed
For Divine help
But the killing did not stop

Greed overlooked all needs
And animal, human, and plants
Had no chance against this
Apocalyptic enemy

Animals were killed for the thrill
Air and water polluted
As the quality of life for all was diluted
Forests were burnt down
As the ashes contaminated
The atmosphere and ground
But not a sound could be heard to protest
Because the virus killed off all of our best
Mass genocide
Of all kinds of human beings
That did not know how to coincide
And rise up against what they were seeing

It started as a tiny thought
In a tiny man
That forgot to rationalize
Or even understand

That destroying the earth
Would eventually destroy
His own land

Still man rejected God
And protected nothing

But the earth fought back
And became green again

New species were born
But none were of man
For the earth had cured itself of
The virus

Divine Purpose

We are all God's children
So that makes us brothers and sisters
Because we are brothers and sisters
We should love and take care of each other

We do not have God's infinite wisdom
Therefore God gave us each other
So that we may share our skills
Knowledge and experience

Thus we may see more
Do more
Know more
And be more
Than we ever could be by ourselves

God gave us a large home to share
The great planet earth
If we do not take care of our home
We will have no place to stay

God gave each one of us time and space
Therefore giving us
Exactness and uniqueness

No one knows everything...
But each of us has something special to give
Every man every woman every child

There is nothing in life that does not serve
A Divine purpose

Even problems have their place
In the developmental plan of life
Like the body must exercise to become strong
So must the spirit and the mind exercise
With the problems of life

Every day we live is a blessing
But our final blessing will not be determined
By how many things we have obtained
Or the status given to us by humankind

Our final blessing will be determined by
How well we have taken care of each other
As brothers and sisters
In the service of Divine wisdom

Thank you for reading this book.
May God bless you and your loved ones.

Remember, I See You!

About the Author

saac Brown Jr was born in the small town of Salem, New Jersey in 1952. He has witnessed many things during his sixty-eight years of life. The joy of family and friends juxtaposed against living among financially struggling families, including his own, has framed insights captured in this book. Friends, neighbors, and the world around him, all piqued his curiosity to understand why people do the things they do. At an early age, he had a disposition towards observing, studying, and writing about people. Thus, Isaac was inspired to write his first poem when he was eleven years old. The poem described his emotional reaction to the assassination of President John F. Kennedy.

Isaac graduated Magna Cum Laude with a Psychology degree from Widener University located in Chester, Pennsylvania. He retired from working almost thirty-nine years in a major corporation. But Isaac did not retire from life. He went back to his first love, creative writing.

Isaac's emotional and intellectual character has been formed by witnessing the civil rights movement of the sixties and seventies, the many wars fought for "freedom," various national and world atrocities, to the very personal observations of those around him. The poems in this book reflect his reaction and insights into the aforementioned. He has stated that it can be both a curse and a blessing to have the gift of "I See You."